THE BOY WHO WAS A BEAR

"A genuinely imaginative writer ... opening parallel worlds within our own... Ideal for seven-pluses who want a challenge but are still discouraged by long books, this is one of the most haunting books I have read this year." *The Times*

A bear cub sheds his skin to become a boy in this magical story.

Charles Ashton has spent most of his life in Scotland. He now lives in the village where he was brought up and his two younger children go to the school that he went to. His books for young people include the Dragon Fire trilogy – *Jet Smoke and Dragon Fire* (shortlisted for both the Guardian Fiction Award and the WHSmith Mind Boggling Books Award), *Into the Spiral* and *The Shining Bridge* – as well as several stories for younger readers, of which *The Giant's Boot* was shortlisted for the 1995 Smarties Book Prize.

D0994214

Books by the same author

The Giant's Boot
Ruth and the Blue Horse
The Snow Door

For older readers

Billy's Drift
Into the Spiral
Jet Smoke and Dragon Fire
The Shining Bridge

THE BOY WHO WAS A BEAR

CHARLES ASHTON

Illustrations by

PETER MELNYCZUK

WALKER BOOKS

AND SUBSIDIARIES

LONDON • BOSTON • SYDNEY

For Anne Robertson
with thanks – not only for the story

First published 1997 by Walker Books Ltd
87 Vauxhall Walk, London SE11 5HJ

This edition published 1997

2 4 6 8 10 9 7 5 3

Text © 1997 Charles Ashton
Illustrations © 1997 Peter Melnyczuk

This book has been typeset in Plantin.

Printed in England by Clays Ltd, St Ives plc

British Library Cataloguing in Publication Data
A catalogue record for this book is
available from the British Library.

ISBN 0-7445-5454-3

Contents

Chapter 1

It was a cold spring and a wet summer, the year we were born – Lala, and Rumba, and Kamanda, and I. That was what drove our mother lower and lower down the mountain slopes, down into the maple forests and to the open fields at the edge of the forests, and into sight of the Light-at-Night place.

They were dusk-time forays we made, over the fences and into the swishing oatfields, sometimes into the rich-earth places near the men-people dens, where the sweetest food was to be had. Dangerous forays that always ended with the terrible bang! of a gun and a fearful dash back up the slopes.

I was the one who told her, "Mother, we don't need to live in such danger. Teach us the skin-change magic, then we could leave our skins and go into the Light-at-Night place looking like men-people. We could eat as much as we wanted in safety, and then go back to the forest, put on our skins, and be bear-people again."

Our mother laughed and cuffed me over on

to my back and told me I didn't understand anything. "If we ate the food of the men-people," she told us, "we should become men-people ourselves and stop being bear-people. Our skins wouldn't fit us any more and we should always have to wear men-people skins, which are soft and smooth as a mushroom cap, and tear open if they touch so much as a bramble-thorn. I will teach you the skin-change magic because my mother taught it to me, but I don't see much use for it. These are not the old days, and the men-people don't want to speak to the bear-people any more."

I knew that men-people skin was not much use, but I did want to take off my bear-skin and feel what it was like. Of course I couldn't until our mother had shown us how, and that was why I kept pestering her about it. But "not this side of winter" was her reply. "Wait till the new spring comes."

What made her change her mind? I shall never know. Perhaps somehow she knew she would die before the new spring came. I understand now why she was always so hungry, though of course I didn't then. Four cubs was too many, and that and the bad summer exhausted her. Perhaps that was how she knew she would die. Poor Mother.

The day when she did show us the skin-change magic was a grey day of autumn, but it had been a good day of hunting. We had found a young sheep tangled in a bramble bush. Mother had killed it and we had feasted! "Too much blood," she had grumbled then, and led us off to grub up swollen mustard roots.

After that she was in a very good humour, and at nightfall led us down to the edge of the open meadows where we could see the yellow glow of the Light-at-Night place (the men-people call it the town). She gazed down at it for some while, then told us, "It must be where you can see the men-people places. Otherwise the men-people skin will not want to come out."

That was how it felt. It wasn't like taking our bear-people skin off: it was more like letting the men-people skin come out from inside. I can't explain it properly and, anyway, it seems so long ago now, I have almost forgotten what it felt like. One moment we were five bears at the edge of the forest; the next, we were looking down at our strange, silky, men-people skins, feeling them with our strange soft men-people paws, and laughing and exclaiming in astonishment.

"It's just like mushroom caps!" I laughed – "though not so squashy. Does it get slimy when it's wet, like mushrooms?"

But our mother did not laugh. She gave us many instructions. She told us we must take care of our bear-people skins and wrap them up with the fur outwards and hide them where they could not be found. She warned us of terrible dangers. If the skins were found they might be stolen. If they were damaged we could never again return to them and would have to stay men-people forever. If they grew cold and stiffened we would never be able to put them on again, though as long as there was just so much as a paw-fist of warmth left in them we could return to them. So we must roll them up well to keep the warmth in, and cover them well with dead grass and leaves and weigh them down with a rock and mark the place with dung.

Our mother showed us the skin-change magic but she would not let us use it. She made us change back into our bear-people skins almost straight away. We were too young, she told us.

Lala and Rumba and, to begin with, Kamanda, were sensible, and obeyed our mother. I did not. One evening, during a foray into the oatfields, I left the others eating and went to sit looking down at the Light-at-Night place. I grew dreamy and started to wonder what it would be like down there, walking among the men-people and listening to them with my ears as they made thoughts with their mouths. The bear-people don't tell each other things with their mouths: we don't make words. Our mouths are for eating and growling and whining with. We make thoughts with our hearts. But our mother had told us that the men-people told each other things by putting thoughts into their mouths and then catching the mouth-thoughts by listening to them with their ears. My brother and sisters thought this was very funny and then forgot about it, but the thought of it would not go out of my head.

The others were all out of sight, so I kept my eyes fixed on the men-people place, and tore softly at my belly as we had been taught, and let the men-people skin come out. I was in a hurry and not as careful as I should have been. I tore up a few oat-stalks and threw them over the bear-people skin, but I couldn't find a stone to cover it with. However, I did remember to make dung and left it close to the skin where I should be able to smell it again easily. Then I crept off through the oatfield.

How strange everything seemed! I have forgotten so much, but I do remember how I could feel everything through my hands and feet instead of with my nose and ears and whiskers and the air around me. At the same time I felt almost blind and almost deaf, and almost without sense of smell. And I remember how the oat-stalks scratched the soft skin on my legs and my bottom and my belly!

I didn't get very far. There was a noise like wind and the sound of beating on the ground, and a dark thing was careering towards me at awful speed. I cried out and tried to run, but it was no use.

It was my mother, of course, and she was furious. She bowled me over and cuffed me and then cuffed me and bowled me over. She even showed her teeth at me. I scampered back the way I had come, but I was in such a panic from seeing her teeth that I couldn't even smell where I had left my dung until I put my foot in it, squelch.

But I had not learnt my lesson. Not long after this, in the dusk of a day when we had been coming down to the tied-up-dead-tree fences between the forest and the open meadows, Kamanda and I had stayed behind at a patch of delicious blackberries. Lala and Rumba and our mother had gone off out of earshot.

"Let's take our skins off," I told her, "and go down to the Light-at-Night place."

Kamanda was horrified that I still wanted to do this after the terrible growling I had had the time before, but I persuaded her that our mother was being an old fusspot, and after I had told her what it was like going through the oatfield with only the soft tickly men-people skin on, she started giggling, and then became curious, and finally agreed to go with me.

We took off our bear-people skins, and Kamanda made me do it properly and carefully this time, hiding them well out of sight. Then we made dung so that we would know exactly where they were hidden, and we were off.

Chapter 2

We went by the meadow, and we squeaked with delight at the feel of the damp spongy grass between our naked toes. But my, it had become cold, and poor Kamanda was shivering by the time we reached the far-end fence. I beckoned her to follow, and we tiptoed down a track in the gathering dark towards the Light-at-Night place.

It's quite hard now to remember how it looked to me that first night as we crept through, slipping from shadow to shadow, crouching behind wagons and gates and barrels. How tall and heavy, how straight and square the walls were! I can't explain. I had grown up in the forest, where everything is curved or crooked. The buildings of the town amazed me with their straightness and squareness. And how hard and flat everything seemed! No yielding mould or moss to put your feet on, or the lovely shapes of rock pressing against your paws: only tight-packed stones or hard-packed earth with a slithery skim of mud on its surface.

It was the cat that upset everything. Up to then our adventure had been very strange but very wonderful. We came to a big building with an opening in the wall – a door left ajar, I know now. There were no yellow lights in this building, but still when we peeped in we could see it was a wide open space with a hard cold floor of amazing flatness. I know now this building was a dairy. There were stone ledges along the walls and strange shapes on the ledges – cans and churns and creamers and strainers and butter-pats, all piled up ready for the morning. We didn't know any of that, of course, but we smelled the faint smell of stale milk – all smells seemed faint to us with our peculiar pale little noses – and it made us curious. We tiptoed in through the great doorway and over to the strange stone ledges.

And there was the cat. A very big cat, ginger and white – I have since learnt that Goliath is his name and he looks after the dairy. He was sitting, with his paws tucked under him, in a cream-setting pan.

We had only once come face-to-face with a cat before, and that time too it was Kamanda who was the first and got nearest to it. That time it was a cat on a rock on the high fir slopes: not a cat like the town-people cats but a lynx with tufted ears flattened back and very cross at being disturbed, baring its teeth in a terrible snarl and hissing unspeakable things at Kamanda. Our mother noticed and laughed and called us to come over and leave the lynx-ruffian in peace, and the lynx had stalked away without bending his knees and with his back-hairs all up in a trembling plume, looking very dignified.

We had all laughed on that occasion and had a fine romp – I was the lynx, and Kamanda and Lala and Rumba had to pin me down and make me hiss terrible thoughts at them – but on this night, as we stood in our men-people skins in the quiet darkness and strange smell of the men-people place, it was very different. Kamanda was terrified, and her hair – her hair that she had like a horse's tail growing out of her head but nowhere else on her body – her hair all stood out to the sides till it was like the shape of an angry swan's wings in the darkness.

And why was she so terrified? Because Goliath was so friendly! Miaow, he said, and then started purring so loudly that the setting pan rattled and the big cans standing beside it began to vibrate softly. Kamanda was goggle-eyed. She was thunderstruck. She was rooted to the spot. I think I have never seen one of the bear-people or one of the men-people so frightened! Oh, I wish I could laugh about it properly!

Kamanda couldn't help herself. Goliath was sitting there looking as peaceful as a currant bun, and all the pans and cans were rattling with his purring – and Kamanda's hand came up, slowly at first then with sudden speed, and gave poor Goliath such a tremendous bear-cuff about the shoulders that he was rolled right out of the setting pan before he knew what had hit him, and before he could get up the pan had flipped over with a terrible clang and landed on top of him.

Kamanda stepped back in horror. But Goliath is a big strong cat and he was very put out, and half-slithered, half-sprang from under the pan, which toppled and rocked its way to the edge of the stone ledge and then dropped with a ringing dong! on to the floor. By now Goliath was leaping around in a panic among the empty cans, sending them flying in all directions, banging and clanging and echoing like gongs all through that big, empty stone place.

Kamanda, the cat and I all took to our heels and fled tumbling out through the door together, Goliath giving a great cat-skirl as I tripped over him on the threshold.

We parted company there, him skittering off into the darkness, Kamanda and I diving for cover behind a pile of dead-tree pieces. I thought we should lie quiet there for a while, but soon Kamanda started whimpering. She thought it was high time we went back to our mother.

If only we had stayed put for a little longer. But it bothered me to hear Kamanda whimpering and snivelling so, so I got up and took her hand and we crept out from behind our cover, along the wall of a building, round a corner and ... straight into the blinding glare of a light that was floating along under the hand of a tall man!

I know now it wasn't blinding – just an ordinary lamp – but it was the brightest thing we had ever seen at night. And I know too, now, that it was Old Joe Murphy holding the lamp and that he wouldn't hurt a fly: but to us there, in the dark, out of our skins, in a strange place, after the terror of the cat, it seemed like the end of the world.

I know now that Old Joe Murphy roared out, "What, kids is it?" Then, more quietly, "Sweet-Mother-Mary, what are you two doing outside with no clothes on?" And then yelling after us as we scampered off uphill and dived through the fence on to the meadow, "Hey, not up there, bairns, do you not know the place is crawling with bears?" But we were not used to hearing mouth-thoughts and his kindly words sounded to us like snarlings and roarings of the most frightening sort.

We ran and ran, out on to the dark meadow, but we were in a great panic and we had gone off in quite the wrong direction. By the time we had realized we were lost Kamanda was again shivering and chattering her teeth together and making little squeaks and squeals like a cub that wants milk.

It was all left to me to work out where we were and how we should get back, but it took time. We knew our mother would not leave the forest's edge as long as we had not returned, and that was a comforting thought; but I never guessed that that comforting thought could mean something so terrible.

It wasn't Joe Murphy's fault, of course. I understand it all now. All the people in the town knew about the bears which had been coming down to the fields and meadows. They knew we had never hurt any of the men-people or their animals, apart from the young sheep that had been stuck, but they were afraid of us. The bear-people had never known that the men-people were afraid of anything; I only know that now because I have lived with them for so long. Joe Murphy had seen two naked children running up into the meadow where there were bears, and he was afraid for them. He gathered men with dogs and guns and they set off on our trail to rescue us.

Kamanda had just smelled her dung-marker and run off ahead, squealing with relief, into the darkness. But now that we had found our way back to safety, I paused and looked back and felt a tug of regret. We had had a fine adventure, it was true, but I had been ready for more, and now I almost felt I wanted to go back down and continue exploring the Light-at-Night place.

It was as I stood there looking back down the hill that I realized we were being followed.

They were quite near, and I had not heard them: men with lights, men with dogs. Looking for children, not bears. My mother must have heard Kamanda squealing when she found her dung-marker and bear-skin – must have heard that, and seen the men and dogs following us.

I could not see what happened, it was too dark. I heard my mother's growl and felt the slight shaking of the ground as she pounded down from the forest's edge to get between us and the men. I heard the yelp of a dog and I heard the whole night break into terrible crackling bangs. It was not the first time I had heard guns, but it was the first time I had heard them so close, or so many all at once.

I couldn't see what happened, but I knew what it meant; and I felt the last heart-thoughts of Mother and Lala and Rumba as they lay still and died.

The men and their dogs caught up with me

at the top of the meadow. I had not moved from the moment I heard my mother's growl and the sound of the guns. Some of them stayed with me, others went on up into the forest, following Kamanda's trail. I heard no more sound of guns.

Chapter 3

The men seemed kindly, though I was scared of the dogs which they had to hold back from me, whining and slavering at the ends of strong ropes. Someone wrapped something warm and itchy round my shoulders and lifted me off my feet, and so I was carried, still and silent, down to the town-place.

There was great amazement when I was put down to stand on the floor in one of their smoky light-spaces. Of course, no one knew who I was, but also none of them seemed to know *what* I was.

"He's a little Injun," someone said. "That what you are, kid? You a little Injun?"

I stared at him.

I understood the men, understood what they were saying to me. It seems strange now when I think about it, but it didn't seem strange then. The heart-thoughts of the bear-people, and the mouth-thoughts of the men-people, they are the same; that was how I understood them.

One of the men bent down to me, his

hands on his knees, his face thrust forward to my face. Strange he smelled, strange like no living thing ever smelled. I know that smell now, the men-people smell, tobacco-smoke and whisky, but it almost knocked me over then. Still, however bad he smelled, the man was being kind.

"That your sister?" he said. "The little girl? We'll get her back down safely, never worry. That your sister?"

And I understood what he was saying, and my mouth moved and made the sound "Kamanda". It was the same as the heart-thought that meant my sister, and it was the first mouth-thought I made, using my throat and my lips and my tongue: Kamanda. The same name, but made out loud so that you could hear it with your ears.

And then they wanted me to eat, and some of the men-women came in then to see what all the commotion was about, and they crowded round me, rustling and exclaiming in their different voices. These were nicer voices than the men's: not so harsh, higher and softer, and the men-women smelled nicer too, more like living things, but I thought it was strange that they had no legs. I didn't know about skirts then, and thought the men-women only had feet at the end of very long bodies!

The men-women wanted me to eat, but I pressed my lips together and turned my head away even though they tried to squeeze things into my mouth. I may have been a foolish and disobedient cub, but I remembered that much of our mother's instructions. If I ate men-people food I would not be able to put on my bear-skin again. I gazed up through the smoke and the yellow lamplight at the straight branches of the dead-tree roof and wondered that I could see no sky peeping through it.

The men-women had just given up trying to make me eat when someone said, "Here's the Injun"; and the crowd moved aside to let in a tall newcomer with a great mane of black hair.

Apart from his hair he looked the same as the rest of the men-people, but they seemed to think he knew things that they did not. The man looked down at me intently for a while and then said quietly, "That ain't no Indian."

Then all the men-people started talking at once. They seemed to think the man with the black-hair mane had said something very strange. Some of the men seemed to be getting angry with him. But the black-mane man turned round and pushed his way through them till I could no longer see him.

"Ain't no Indian," I heard him say. "Him's one of the bear-people. Best let him go."

Then he was gone and everyone fell silent and turned back to stare at me. I don't know what happened then. I suppose it must have been the shock of hearing what the black-mane man had said. The men-people call it fainting. It hasn't happened to me again and it doesn't happen to the bear-people. What it means is that you close your eyes for a moment and when you open them again you're lying on the ground, or perhaps even somewhere completely different because, if you faint, sometimes the men-people want to carry you away somewhere where you can lie quiet after you've opened your eyes again.

I opened my eyes in a wonderfully soft place on a sort of ledge off the floor. A bed. Two of the men-women were bending over me, one on each side. They were both nice, but one of them had wonderful, soft, watchful eyes like a mother-bear's, and she stroked my strange, soft forehead with her strange, soft hand and made soft noises at me, and I was still gazing at her when I fell asleep.

I felt very strange the next day. They hung skins on me – strange itchy skins that didn't move properly with my body, so that every time my body moved it rubbed against the skin that was wrapped round me. It took me many days to get used to the feeling of clothes.

They tried to get me to eat again, but I would not. One of the men-women who had been with me the night before – not the one with the mother-bear eyes – got angry, but I put my head down and pressed my lips together and closed my eyes.

I sat like that for a long time. I wanted them to stop watching me. I wanted to get back to my skin before it got quite cold – I didn't know how long that would be – so that I could follow after Kamanda and tell her what had happened. I had a ball of sadness in me as heavy as a stone lying on my chest. The men-people were quite nice, but I wanted to go and be myself again and cry for my mother and Lala and Rumba in my own way, curled up somewhere with my sister Kamanda.

Halfway through the morning perhaps, the black-mane man came in again. The other men-people behaved quite strangely towards him. I understand now that he belongs to a different people of the men-people, and they think a lot of the things he says are very funny. It seemed there had been a big argument outside about whether to let him do what he wanted to do. He had got his way in the end, it seemed, but the others still laughed at him.

He took me by the hand and said, "Come outside." And I went, but I still kept my lips pressed together in case any of them tried to put food into my mouth.

The black-mane man went with me on to the meadow where we had come down the night before, and held my hand as we walked up towards the forest. Then he stopped and let go of my hand and said, "Go where you want to go," and turned away to face downhill.

He didn't move from where he was standing, but I knew he meant not to look round to know where I was going. I understood then that he really was different from the other men-people, who all wanted to watch me all of the time. I looked back several times as I went to the top of the meadow and then started working my way along the forest edge, and the black-mane man never moved but stood with his back to me gazing down the hillside.

Before long I smelled my dung-marker, and then I ran. I was full of glee, and gave no more thought to the chance that my skin might have got too cold. Well-covered it had been under leaves and moss, well wrapped on itself with the fur outward, and it only needed to have one paw-fist of warmth left in it. Kamanda had been very careful about how we left our skins.

I came to Kamanda's dung-marker and saw the leaves and mould disturbed where her skin had been. It was gone. She had taken her skin and got away. Good. Then I came to my marker.

I still remember how I looked down at the dead-leaf place in a tree-hollow where I had put my skin, and would not believe what I saw. The place had been disturbed and the skin was gone. There were clear marks among the yellow leaves carpeting the ground where it had been dragged off.

Then a comforting thought came to me: Kamanda had taken my skin with her to keep it warm! All I had to do was follow the trail and I would find it and her.

But I had not gone far when I found it. At first, I thought that an old brown honeycomb had fallen out of a tree and broken apart on the ground and I would be able to feast! I even thought Kamanda must have knocked it down and left it there for me. But it was not a honeycomb, it was my skin, in pieces, chewed up and slavered on by dogs and scattered on the forest floor. I crawled about there gathering the wet pieces, pressing them together into a soggy heap of skin and fur and mixed-up moss, cold, cold as the soil.

The black-mane man was still standing down on the meadow, still as a bare thorn-tree, when I crept out of the forest again with my dead-animal-skin clothes scratching and snagging against my soft men-people skin. I did not know what else to do. I went down to him. I was holding a handful of my own fur and I held it up to him and he looked at it slowly. Then he put his arm round my shoulder briefly and said, "Follow me," and started back down the hill towards the town-place.

The black-mane man left me at one of the dead-tree houses: I don't know if it was the same one where I had spent the night. Men-people came in and out and looked at me and discussed me.

A man told me what had happened the night before, how a mother-bear had charged at them on the meadow and how two young bears had followed her and how all three had been shot. Then the man said, "He's crazy mad, that Injun. He says you was a bear, can you believe that? As if you hadn't been through enough without some crazy Injun putting ideas into your head. I'm truly grieved 'bout your little sister, boy. Ain't no sign of her at all, but there was signs of another young bear up where she went. Ain't like a young bear to go killing kids, but there it is. Don't you worry though, that bear that got away, he won't get through the winter – not a young bear all by himself, no chance. Them bears are all gone now."

I knew the man was trying to be kind, but I couldn't understand why he wanted me to feel glad about Kamanda not getting through the winter. I had to think hard before I realized that he thought I would want the bear to die because it had killed my sister. It was very complicated.

Chapter 4

They pulled my mother's skin off her body, and made it dry and took away its mother-smell and pinned it stretched out on the wall of the place-where-men-drink. The Bar, that place is called, and it's where the men make themselves smell of whisky and tobacco-smoke. Meanwhile I was taken to live with the woman with the mother-bear eyes, the one who had stroked my head till I fell asleep. Her name was Mrs MacKenzie and she was the schoolteacher in the town.

She lived alone and was very quiet and gentle. She said I would have to come to her school and learn things and meet the other boys and girls, but I wouldn't have to do that straight away. I have worked out that as a bear-cub I could have been no more than eight months old, but as one of the men-people I appeared as a boy of, I suppose, nine or ten.

Mrs MacKenzie said I should call her Aunt Janie, and then asked me what my name was. I said, "Bear." It was difficult: the thing is, those heart-thoughts, Kamanda, Lala, Rumba, that meant my sisters and my brother, were only heart-thoughts to me. I don't know the heart-thought that meant me to them. I didn't know my name. The men-people use their names to call to each other to listen to their mouth-thoughts, but the heart-thoughts of the bear-people are for everyone, so the bear-people don't need to call a name out before they make a heart-thought.

So I just said "Bear" to Aunt Janie because I was a bear.

Aunt Janie laughed. "You were certainly bare when you came to live with us," she said. "You had no clothes on at all! But I don't think Bare's a good name. We'll call you Bobby."

Aunt Janie asked me some questions about my family, but I couldn't speak about them, and she didn't try to make me. I never told anyone my secret except for the black-mane man. I knew I had to become one of the men-people, but I also hoped against hope that my sister Kamanda would survive the winter and I would find her again.

In the meanwhile I had to learn to be a boy. It was difficult. For one thing, boys have to use toilets, and I got quite a scolding from Aunt Janie for making a mess on her nice wooden floor. Not that her scoldings were ever that severe.

And then there was eating. The men-people kill nearly all their eating-food in boiling water. The boiling water makes the food hot, and because the food is so hot and they have such soft delicate hands, they can't pick it up, and of course they can't stick their mouths in it either because then they would hurt their lips. So they have to use funny little bits of twisted metal and wood to pick up their hot food and put it into their mouths. At least that was how it seemed to me. I've learned to use knives and forks and spoons now, though sometimes I daydream that I'm sitting in the sun with my brother and sisters, somewhere far up in the high forests, and telling them about the funny way the men-people eat, and making them roll about with laughter. I daydream like that because it helps me to do all the strange men-people things I'm expected to do.

After a few days, Aunt Janie started leaving me alone a lot of the time. I found out that this was because she had to go off to be the schoolteacher in another building down in the middle of the town.

I tried very hard to behave myself while she was away.

It was all right if I was outside. Sometimes I would spend the day with Old Joe Murphy, who told me wonderful tales about his days at sea – which is a huge flat place where there's so much water there's no room for anything else except the sky. He floated on the sea on a very big log called the *Flower of Ballyclare*. It must have been very big because he had lots of friends who floated on it with him. Or sometimes I spent the day with the black-mane man, who was called Running Deer. He didn't speak much, but he would take me up into the forests and let me climb trees and look for signs of my sister. He didn't say he was letting me do that, but I know he knew that's what I was doing.

So that was all right, those days outside; but sometimes when I was left in the house I did get into trouble. I couldn't work out how things wouldn't stay in their place when I touched them. They were always falling off or toppling over. It was one day when I knocked over the wooden box in the sleeping-room – it was full of men-people dead-skins and Aunt Janie called it a wardrobe – that I discovered the mirror.

I had been sitting on top of the wardrobe-box and then it toppled over and I landed in a heap on the floor and then a bit of the wardrobe-box seemed to swing round somehow, and there I was face-to-face with a little brown boy-cub with bushy hair and staring black eyes. It was amazing. I was still looking at him when Aunt Janie came home, and when she had scolded me a little as she always did and stood the wardrobe up again, she showed me that it was just myself in the flat cold skin of the mirror. Of course I had seen reflections before, but never as clear or as real-looking as this.

I spent a lot of my time looking at myself after that, and Aunt Janie laughed and said I was very vain and should be ashamed of myself. But soon after this I discovered that she stood in front of the mirror too, every day, and touched her face and did things to her hair. But when I told her she was vain she said it was all right for her because she was a lady. Anyway she was so beautiful I could understand why she stood and looked at herself. I wasn't beautiful. I was brown and bushy and I didn't look like the bear I should have looked like.

I didn't go far from the town, not even when I was with Running Deer. Sometimes Aunt Janie stayed at home and took me about the town and showed me things, sometimes into the fields and woods round about. There was one track that wound off up among the trees and rocks of the steep hillside. Aunt Janie took me up it a little way until we came to a creamy water that was flowing down beside the track. Just where we stopped the stream dived into a hole in the ground and disappeared from view. The water looked strange and thick and yellow and it smelled unpleasant, and it was not cold as water should be.

"It comes from a hot sulphur-spring," Aunt Janie told me. "Sulphur's a kind of yellow rock they used to dig out of the caves up there – they wanted it for making matches and killing bugs on vegetables and things like that. It makes the water that colour – it doesn't smell very nice, does it?" Then she said sternly, "I want you to promise me you won't go any further up this track. The sulphur caves are dangerous. My husband went up there, and he never came back."

I wanted to know if My Husband meant her brother or what, because she seemed very sad about it, but she said it wasn't her brother. She paused and seemed to think a bit, then she said, "Don't you remember your daddy? – well, that's what my husband was like."

Well! Now I did understand why the sulphur caves were dangerous, or I thought I did. I had never seen my daddy, but we had heard of him – he was a great scary monster-bear that lived up in the high rock-clefts, and we knew to keep out of his way! That was before I found out that the men-people men were practically all Daddies and they all lived with their own cubs. That was very funny! Lala and Kamanda would have laughed their ears off about that! But I didn't know all this at the time, and I thought the sulphur caves must be dangerous because of the My-Husband-Daddy that had gone there and not come out again.

So: Aunt Janie taught me to use the toilet-closet out at the back of the house; she stood over me through long, yawning, messy mealtimes as I learned to sit up at a table and eat food by holding it with the twisted-metal-bits in my hand; she made sure I had begun to remember that I shouldn't suck my toes or scratch my bottom when anyone was watching – and after all that, she thought I was ready to go to school.

At school I discovered that the men-people didn't just make mouth-thoughts, but they used little white sticks which they held in their hands to make pictures of the mouth-thoughts on thin flat stones. It was called writing. It was very funny, and for some reason I found it very easy, and soon Aunt Janie said I was the best writer in the class, and made more beautiful mouth-thoughts on the flat stones than she had ever seen in her school before. Except that when I was at school I wasn't allowed to call her Aunt Janie, I had to call her Mrs MacKenzie like the other men-people-cubs. (That's what I call them to myself: I know to call them boys and girls out loud, but I still think of them as men-people-cubs.)

They were nice to me, the other boys and girls. Every single one of them. I don't know why: I know that sometimes they were not at all nice to each other. But they were always nice to me, and they were always nice to each other when I was around.

I made particular friends with one of them. He was just like a brother. He was called Sandy. Perhaps the name reminded me of Kamanda.

Chapter 5

"You ever gone shooting, Bobby?" Sandy said to me one winter's day.

I did not know what Sandy meant by "gone shooting."

"I got a gun," Sandy said. "We can take turns with it."

I knew what guns were, and I didn't like the sound of this at all. But I could see that Sandy wasn't afraid, and I had learned by this time that boy-cubs were never supposed to show if they were afraid, so I said "Sure", and we set off up the hillside on the bright-snow ground

"Remember..." Aunt Janie called as I went out.

"Don't go near the sulphur caves!" I called back to her. As if I needed any warning!

"I shot a hare once," Sandy told me, in a big puffed-up-throat voice. I could see he meant something very important. "What have you shot?"

I shrugged. I didn't really know how to answer. "Hares are very fast," I said.

"This'n was sitting still as still," Sandy said. "But he was a white'n, you could hardly see'n in the snow – and I shot'n clean through the heart."

I felt a shiver passing down my spine. I couldn't tell how Sandy's gun was exactly used – it was another of the twisted metal-and-wood things that the men-people have. But it was big, and I knew it had been a gun that killed my mother and Lala and Rumba.

Well, I didn't exactly find out, but I gave Sandy a very big scare. It's very funny when I think about it now. It was ptarmigans we had seen, up on a rocky height, and Sandy picked up his gun and held it in a strange way and made a strange twisted face at it, and suddenly there was the most terrible bang that made my head ring inside and made me shriek like – I don't know what. But I think the shriek scared me even more than the bang, and I ran and ran until I bumped into a tree and it knocked me down.

That stopped me being so scared, because

it made my nose too sore for me to be scared properly. So I got up and went back to where we had been standing. There I saw Sandy's gun lying on the ground. There must have been something very hot at the end of it because it had melted itself down through the snow. But there was no Sandy.

After a little, Sandy came creeping back through the trees, peeping round each one as he came. "What's the matter, Sandy?" I said.

"Where d'you learn to make a god-darn noise like that?" he said in a trembling voice. "You near frightened me half to death!"

If Sandy hadn't let me see he was frightened, I wouldn't have answered him, because boy-cubs weren't supposed to be frightened of anything. But he had, so I said, "The sound of the gun frightened me. My mommy got killed by a gun, see. Ain't frightened of nothing else, though." (That was how I had learned to talk.)

"Me neither, I ain't frightened of nothing," Sandy said. "Nothing 'cept that god-darn screaming noise you made."

That was the end of our shooting-trip. We had had enough excitement for one day. And we didn't go shooting again.

"Who was your mommy, anyway?" Sandy asked as we went homewards.

I said nothing then. But later on, after we had had our supper with Aunt Janie and I was seeing Sandy back to his house, dawdling through the town in the snow-silver darkness, we passed the place-where-men-drink, and I stopped and pushed the door open a little, and pointed through the smoke to the great skin stretched on the wall with its head hanging down and its big snarling teeth.

"That there's my mommy," I said quietly.

Just then someone roared at us to get out and go home, and we cut and ran. When we stopped running Sandy pushed me and said, "You're a right cook you are, Bobby! Always cooking up some joke. But I best be getting along home now or that old bear on the wall, that's gonna be just how my mommy looks when she sees me – all big teeth and not much smiling neither!"

Sandy and I were better friends than ever when we said goodbye that night, because we had both been frightened together. But we had also said that we weren't frightened of anything else. Of course, we were both boasting; but somehow we knew that one day we would have to prove to each other that we could be very brave as well.

The winter passed, and spring and summer came; and in the autumn we got the chance.

In the spring – the first spring after I became one of the men-people – all the men were speaking of something very unusual which had been seen in the forest.

"Not that far from the town neither," Old Joe Murphy said. "I've never seen anything like it, as God's my judge. A bear it is for sure – but bright yellow, yellow as a maple tree in autumn."

"Na – yellower'n that," someone else said.

"Yellowest thing I've ever seen – bar a lemon skin. It's a lemon-skin bear!"

It was a great mystery, and the men argued about it for weeks on end. Some of them wanted to go and hunt the yellow bear and bring its skin back, but somehow no one got around to it, so for the time being it was left in peace.

As for me, I didn't care much whether they shot the yellow bear or left it in peace, I'm afraid. All I could think of was what Kamanda would have thought about it if she had been alive to see it. But I knew she had probably slept herself into the cold, somewhere up on the mountain slopes in the winter, and would never wake up again. I was quite interested in the yellow bear, but I was interested as one of the men-people, not one of the bear-people.

It was Aunt Janie who had the wonderful idea about the yellow bear. Aunt Janie was very clever – that was why she was the schoolteacher – but the men didn't listen to her all that much. That was why it was just

Sandy and I who heard her idea, months later, at the beginning of the autumn, one evening when the three of us were sitting outside her house in the late sunshine.

"People have forgotten," she said, "because it's been so long since anyone worked the sulphur mines. Those old caves up there are full of sulphur fumes. They'd turn anything yellow if it was in there for long enough. That bear's spent the winter in the sulphur caves. The fumes have turned its fur yellow."

When we heard Aunt Janie's guess about the strange bear living in the sulphur caves, I looked at Sandy and Sandy looked at me: and we both knew that we had to go up to those caves and see if it was true, just to prove that we weren't frightened of anything.

Chapter 6

One grey Saturday morning when the air was all lit up by the yellow leaves of maples we set off up the forbidden track beside the strange-smelling not-cold stream.

"Should'a brought my gun," Sandy grumbled.

"I'd scream," I grinned.

The path climbed up into steep gorges of tree-grown rock, and everything was very silent, apart from the occasional whisper of the stream as it went in and out of the rocks. People didn't come this way.

"You scared, Bobby?" Sandy said to me after some time. "We could always go back."

"I ain't scared," I answered.

The rocky gorges were very high, and it was gloomy and damp. The maple trees here had brown leaves, not yellow ones, and that made it even gloomier. The air smelled rotten. Neither Sandy nor I spoke now.

The track led through a gap, like a missing tooth, in a rocky ridge. Once we had passed through the gap, it was suddenly not so dark.

We were in a wide open space, all pale yellow, with low cliffs all round, and broken-down grey-brick-places and big rusty shapes scattered – more of the men-people twisted-metal things. No plants grew. In the cliffs were caves, dark gaping holes, all wrong somehow, and everything full of the bad-smelling air. This was no bear-place. There were no marks on the pale mud. "Aunt Janie was wrong," I said. "Ain't nothing here."

Sandy let out a long sigh. I think it was relief. "Well, we had a look," he said. "Best get off home now."

"Better have a look in them caves," I said. "Seeing as we're here."

"But you said yourself," Sandy said, "as how Mrs MacKenzie was wrong."

"You scared, Sandy?" I said.

"No, no, Bobby, I ain't scared."

"What then?"

"Well," he said, "we only came to look for that old yellow bear, not to look around in any caves. That ain't brave, looking around inside them caves, that's just foolish. Mr MacKenzie, he came to look around inside them caves – he never came back, now, did he? We came to look for that yellow bear and he's not here, so now we get back down the track, right?"

"All right then, Sandy," I said with a smile. I was pretty sure he felt scareder than I did, so that was all right. But I couldn't help adding, "Wouldn't do no harm to call in though, would it. Don't have to go in them caves – just stand outside and holler, see if Mr Bear's home."

I was teasing Sandy really, I didn't think there was any bear there. I just wanted him to know I was braver than him even though I didn't like guns.

So that was what we did. There were six caves altogether, and we went to each one and called, "Hey, Mr Bear! You home? Come on out and say hello!" By the time we had got round four of the caves and got no reply, I could see Sandy was feeling a lot braver; he was shouting and hollering even louder than me by then. The strange-smelling air was strong in the mouths of the caves; it made our eyes prickle and it made us cough. So we shouted and coughed, and Sandy was capering about and bawling, "Hey, Mr Bear, come out! Come out and say Hellowallawall-awallawalla!"

"Come on, Sandy," I said. "That's about enough now."

But Sandy wouldn't leave off now, he'd become so brave, and he went on wallawallawalla-ing, and jumping up and down and throwing stones in...

And then we heard it. It was a grunt. A grunt from very far in that cave, but it echoed as it came out, so it was both louder and softer, somehow, than it should have been. And Sandy stopped hollering, and suddenly he looked very pale, though that might have been because of the yellow dust in the cave-entrances. And suddenly he yelled, "Run, Bobby, run! Run for your life!"

And we were off. Well, we'd both heard that grunt, and a bear-grunt coming out of a cave has got to mean "Run" to young boy-cubs!

And yet – it was the first bear-grunt I'd heard for nearly a year, and I can't say exactly how it made me feel, but it didn't make me feel quite like running. A bit, yes, especially as I was thinking of that scary Daddy-bear I'd thought was there. But mostly it was Sandy who made me feel like running – and he was slithering off like a hare across that wide pale space with the rusty metal-things, and screaming and bawling; and so I followed him, but not quite as fast, and he was just about out of the tooth-gap gateway when I slowed down and turned round and took a look and...

And there was the yellow bear coming running out of the cave, charging the way a bear charges, but no colour of any living bear I'd even dreamed of – yellower than maple-leaves, yellow as lemons – and I stopped. I suppose I should have been scared, and I think Sandy must have turned round just before he got to the gateway-place because I heard him screaming at me to come on. But I couldn't run. No, not if it had been the biggest scariest Daddy-bear there was, I couldn't have run...

It was quite a big bear. I didn't think as big as my mother was, but I couldn't really remember. Certainly no Daddy-bear, I could see that right away. But that wasn't what made me stop running. I stopped because it was Kamanda.

She'd grown of course. That wasn't any wonder. It had been a good summer and there must have been plenty to eat. And she had that weird yellow fur that no living bear should have. But it was her, and I think I knew it from the very instant I saw her rushing out after us – no, before that, from the moment I heard that grunt – no, even before that: because of what Aunt Janie had said, about the not-cold water coming from the hot spring in the sulphur cave, and about how it was the sulphur-caves that had turned the bear yellow. The crafty one! That was how she had survived the winter all by herself: she had slept in the cave with the hot spring!

I don't know when she realized it was me. She had been charging. She'd seen a couple of men-people-cubs coming to annoy her and she would have been chasing them away; and if they hadn't made it out through the gateway-place she might have killed one of them, just to teach them. But she slowed down suddenly and skidded a little on the pale mud, and then she stopped; and I could see a puzzled look about her, and she swung her head from side to side – stupid yellow head – and then she didn't look puzzled any more, and I felt her heart-thought coming out over me, and just at that moment the sun found a hole in the clouds and came shining down, warm and queer, pale golden everywhere on the sulphur-mud.

"Kamanda," I said. "Kamanda – Kamanda."

I couldn't say anything else.

And Kamanda came up to me, and put her nose up against my nose and then sniffed down to my neck and down over my hands, and I felt her heart-thought strong, strong like the sun; but there was something puzzled too, because she was thinking there was something just as queer about me as I was thinking there was about her in her yellow coat.

And then I realized what it was. It was my mouth-thought. She had never heard that sound, Kamanda, before, and she didn't understand it. And she didn't understand how it was me standing there, yet giving out no heart-thought.

Because I'd forgotten. I didn't know how to make heart-thoughts any more. And when I wanted to, to let her know everything that had happened to me and how I had missed her and searched for her, all I could think of was mouth-thoughts, and I knew they were no use.

We managed a bit. She rolled over and

invited me to romp, and I leaped on top of her and we rolled a bit, but I could feel she was uneasy about my soft little men-people body, and she was trying hard not to hurt me. But then I sat up, and so did she; and that was when we saw Sandy coming walking timidly towards us. And then Kamanda leaped to her feet with a startled kind of grunt and then turned suddenly and ran back into the cave with just a single glance back at me.

I am a boy now, I know that, and I shall grow up to be a man. I should like to be a tall straight man like Running Deer, but I know my hair will always be pale-brown and fuzzy and I shall never have a magnificent black mane like his. Perhaps I shall be a Daddy-man when I grow big and live with my cubs like the other men-people fathers. I know I shall never be a bear again. I am quite sad, but not too sad.

I see Kamanda often, and that makes me happy. Kamanda hardly ever goes to the place where we met, the pale open-space with the rusty-metal shapes among the low cliffs: there is a small back-entrance to the caves, and she only came out the other way that day because she heard us boys and wanted some peace.

I don't go into the rusty-metal open-space either. When I visit her, I go to her small cave entrance amongst the heather-grown rocks.

Oh, I visit her a lot. Aunt Janie doesn't mind. Often I stay with her when she isn't foraging, curled up together as we once used to be. Sandy is a little scared of me now, but we are still good friends. He believes I am scared of nothing!

No one in the town will harm Kamanda. No one knows my secret, even now, apart from Running Deer, but the people say I have "a way about me" and understand animals. But it's not just because of me that Kamanda will always be safe from their guns: they also like to boast to strangers about the yellow bear that lives near to their town and hurts no one.

Kamanda has made her den in the sulphur caves for two winters now. This last winter she gave birth to two cubs – I am an uncle! – and they are both as yellow as she. Will she teach them, I wonder, to take off their bear-skins and wander amongst the men-people? I think not. Something has happened to Kamanda.

When I found I had forgotten how to make heart-thoughts to her, I tried to get Kamanda to take her bear-skin off so that she could be one of the men-people for a while and we could make mouth-thoughts to each other. I took her forepaw and stroked the claws down her strange yellow chest, but she would not make the magic to take off her skin.

I don't think she had forgotten. I don't know quite how it is, because her heart-thoughts seem confused, or I am too human to understand them: I think she has been telling me she can't take her skin off because it has turned yellow. I certainly know that Kamanda is very proud of her lemon-yellow fur. She has become vain! One day I shall get a big mirror and carry it up to her! It may be because she has become vain that she won't take her skin off, but I can't be sure. It may be because the sulphur has killed the magic that would let her change. I don't think any of the bear-people would make their den in a sulphur-cave from choice: it was because of her fear after that terrible night when our mother and Lala and Rumba were killed and I was lost.

It may be she won't take her skin off because she has become like our mother: careful, always careful. Well, at least I still have her. People look at us strangely, watching from a distance as we meet and touch noses. Aunt Janie scolds me when I come back to the house with my arms and legs bleeding after a romp with my nephews. They get excited and forget to be careful with me and then Kamanda has to cuff them to remind them.

I don't know their names. I shall never

know their names. I call them Bill and Buster, but those are men-people mouth-thoughts. I shall never know their real names because I have forgotten how to make heart-thoughts.

Or, no: "never" is a long word. It is a man-word – and a word only, not a proper thought. "Never" has no meaning. I hope to live many years with my sister Kamanda. Perhaps, as those years go by, I shall remember how to make heart-thoughts again.

THE STONE THAT GREW
Enid Richemont

Katie finds the stone in an old box in the loft. It doesn't look like much at first, but then it does something amazing: it grows! Katie thinks it's wonderful. What's more, it's hers and she's not going to share it; it's bad enough having to share Mum with her little stepbrother, Jake. It might even be a way of getting in with Sarah and her gang. Meanwhile the stone continues to grow ... and grow!

THE SNOW DOOR
Charles Ashton

On the train to school, Barbara is writing a story about the Pleasant Land which is reached through a magic doorway. But at a certain point she always gets stuck. One day, after a heavy snowstorm, she and her fellow traveller, Miss English, set out on skis for the station. Skiing across country, they come across an old postman lying in the snow. While Miss English goes for help, Barbara has to keep the postie awake by telling him her story. Then the tale takes on a strange and magical life of its own...

MEET ME BY THE STEELMEN
Theresa Tomlinson

At the heart of Meadowhall shopping centre, the site of an old steelworks, stand three giant bronze statues: the steelmen. Stevie can't take his eyes off them; he even claims they move and speak. Jenny, his older sister, thinks he's imagining things – and yet there *is* something strange about the statues. Overnight they seem to change somehow. Could it be they're haunted by steelworkers from the past?

LETTERS FROM A MOUSE
Herbie Brennan

dear reader
i am s. mouse of hayes bros. ltd.
office supplies. i write letters and
answer the phone at night. but right
now im in trouble. a man rang and
asked for a brief case big enough to
hold half a million pounds in unmarked
5 pound notes. i smell a rat. can you
help me solve the mystery?

Can you help a small mouse solve a big mystery? Read
his lively letters and see if you can crack the case!